THE SECRET LIFE OF MS WIZ

What the reviewers have said about *Ms Wiz*:

"Every time I pick up a Ms Wiz, I'm totally spellbound . . . a wonderfully funny and exciting read." *Books for Keeps*

"Hilarious and hysterical."
Susan Hill, *Sunday Times*

"Terence Blacker has created a splendid character in the magical Ms Wiz. Enormous fun."
The Scotsman

"Sparkling zany humour . . . brilliantly funny."
Children's Books of the Year

Titles in the Ms Wiz series

Terence Blacker

THE SECRET LIFE OF MS WIZ

Illustrated by Tony Ross

MACMILLAN
CHILDREN'S BOOKS

First published 2002 by Macmillan Children's Books
a division of Macmillan Publishers Limited
20 New Wharf Road, London N1 9RR
Basingstoke and Oxford
www.panmacmillan.com

Associated companies throughout the world

ISBN 0 333 99460 4

A CIP catalogue record for this book is available from
the British Library.

Typeset by Intype London Ltd
Printed and bound in Great Britain by Mackays of Chatham plc, Kent

Dear Reader

It is now several years since I first
received a visit from someone who
called herself Ms Wiz. She was a
rather unusual person, and she could
sometimes be quite annoying, but
down the years she has become a
very good friend of mine.

Now, something rather odd has
happened. Ms Wiz has asked me
whether, for the first and last time, she
could tell her own story. She said it
was all very well for me to sit here,
telling the world of all the things she
had done, and she wasn't
complaining (although, according to

her, my knowledge of magic is a bit dodgy, I should never have mentioned her age and I've written far too much about Herbert the rat).

But there are some stories, Ms Wiz told me, that are so strange and so private that only a true paranormal operative can tell them.

I am not a true paranormal operative. The fact is, I've never turned anyone into a warthog, my experience of time travel is extremely limited, and I make a mess of the simplest magic trick.

So it is time for me to step aside and let Ms Wiz tell you all about her secret life and the weirdest thing that has ever happened to her during her weird, weird lifetime.

Terence Blacker

Weird? My life? What on earth is he talking about?

No, the fact is that my writer has never quite understood me. I look much younger than he says I do, I'm quite a lot prettier, too. The pictures make my hair look spiky when in fact it has a gentle, natural curl to it, like a wave of dark loveliness. And I'm always *in control of my magic – except when I'm not, which is very rare.*

You, my readers, my public, deserve to hear the truth from the one who knows. So here, at last, it is.

Welcome to my own, personal, secret life.

Ms Wiz

CHAPTER ONE

Beagle Bad

If you are, or have ever been, a
paranormal operative, you will know
what it feels like when something
magical is about to happen. You feel
tense. Your head is woozy, as if you
have drifted off into a dream. From
deep within you, there is a low hum.
It gets louder and louder until people
all around you start noticing it.

Then, quite suddenly . . . BLAM!
All is peace and happiness and
loveliness. It's magic time again.

All these things happened to me,
Ms Wiz, on the day that changed my
life for ever. I was in the sitting room,
reading a story to my little boy,
William. He was wriggling around on

my lap like a dog with fleas.

There was tension. There was the wooziness in my head as if I had drifted off into a dream. A low humming noise was in the air. Normally I'm in control of these things but on this occasion something very odd was happening. I was not in control at all. The humming noise was coming from outside me. Someone else was causing the spell.

"Dolores!" At the very moment when I was beginning to wonder what exactly was going on, I heard the voice of my husband Brian. He was in the kitchen, doing the ironing. "Dolores, something rather unusual has landed in the garden."

"Unusual?" I said, without showing any particular interest. My husband is the kindest, sweetest man in the world but he tends to find

quite a lot of things unusual – the colour of the tie worn by a TV newscaster, for example, or the amount of rainfall in one day, or the way cornflakes go stale if you don't seal them up properly.

"It seems to be a rather large white bird," Brian was saying. "It's not a seagull, so far as I can judge, and it's definitely not a chicken. It may be an owl but I'm almost certain that it's an eagle."

The humming grew louder. William slipped off my lap and ran into the kitchen. "Beagle," he was shouting. "Me see beagle!"

I heard Brian correcting William in the quiet, careful way of his. "Not a beagle, little one. A beagle's a hunting dog. This is a great, white eagle."

A great white eagle? It could only mean one thing. Without a word, I stood up and scurried through the kitchen, past Brian and the Wiz Kid.

"What's that humming noise I can hear?" Brian called out. "I hope this isn't one of your spells. I've told you a thousand times. No magic. You are not Ms Wiz when you are in this house. You are Mrs Dolores Arnold."

I opened the back door. There, on the lawn, was an eagle of pure, dazzling white. Entirely unafraid, it began walking towards me. I smiled and opened my arms wide.

"Hello, Dad," I said.

As I spoke, the bird's feathers seemed to fluff out, then grow hazy, until there was no longer an eagle on the lawn but a swirling cloud of smoke, catching the rays of the sun.

"Did you say 'Dad'?" asked Brian, who was standing at the kitchen door, holding William's hand.

"Bad," said the Wiz Kid. "Beagle bad."

The cloud was beginning to take the shape of a person. A tall, elderly man, wearing a white suit and carrying a cane walking stick stepped through the smoke and walked towards me in a stiff, straight-backed way.

"Father." I hugged him gently and kissed him on both cheeks.

When I stepped back to look at him, he cleared his throat. "I am also your king."

I hesitated for a moment. The truth is, I've never been too happy with the whole kings and queens business. I believe that we are all equal and giving someone a special name does not make them better than you.

"Dolores?" My father smiled, as if he could tell what was going through my head.

I lowered my head and bent a knee in the quickest of curtsies. "Welcome, Your Majesty," I said.

"Excuse me," said Brian. "Would someone mind telling me exactly what is going on? Who is this man? Why did he arrive as a bird? And what is he doing on my lawn, pretending to be a king?"

My father held out his hand. "The

name's Wisdom," he said. "Arthur, King Wisdom, Master of Magic, Sire of Spells, Peer Extraordinaire and Supreme Sovereign of the Kingdom of Paranormal Magic and Utter Eternal Mystery. I'm your father-in-law."

"And I'm Brian Arnold, School Inspector." Brian shook my father's hand. "Pleased to meet you, Arthur. Or should I say, Dad?"

My father winced. "Arthur will do just fine," he said. Seeing William, he asked, "And who might this be?"

"It's your grandson," I said. "William, our own little Wiz Kid."

My father smiled with pride. "Ah, but is he a true Wisdom of the blood?" he asked.

"William," I said. "Fly a bit for your grandfather."

There was a humming noise, more high-pitched than usual. William spread his arms. His body lifted off the ground and he hovered, smiling proudly, for several seconds, before lowering himself to the ground with a bump.

"Very good," said my father. "That's a Wiz Kid if ever I saw one."

"Actually," said Brian. "He's an Arnold, too. I try to have a little house rule about inappropriate magic."

"Inappropriate? How can magic ever be inappropriate?" My father looked confused.

"Let's have a cup of tea inside," I said quickly.

It was not an easy tea party. William was showing off his latest spells, turning himself into a rabbit, flying around the room on a chair. Brian was becoming increasingly annoyed at this outbreak of magic. My father looked on, a polite smile on his face.

"Have you come far?" Brian asked at one point.

"From beyond the outer reaches of the known universe," said my father. "About a million miles beyond, I believe."

"That's a fair old hike," said Brian. "I have to travel in my line of business, too. These days, in the school inspection lark, you have to motor—"

My father clicked his fingers. In that instant, normal time was stopped. Brian sat as still and silent as a statue. William was immobile on his chair, a few inches from the ceiling.

"Sorry about that," said my father. "But we need to talk privately."

"Brian can be a bit . . . human sometimes," I said.

"He seems a nice enough chap." My father turned to me and fixed me with his piercing blue eyes. "I have decided that it is time for you to come home."

"But I am home."

"Home to your true home, the home of the blood, the family. The Palace of Wisdom needs you."

"Needs me?" I laughed nervously.

"What on earth for?"

"I'm tired, Dolores. After 10,000 years on the throne, I'm beginning to feel rather old. That is why I have decided that you, my daughter, should become the Queen of Wisdom."

"Queen?" My voice was a whisper. "I-I'm not sure about all that. What I believe is that we are all equal and giving someone a special name does not—"

My father interrupted me by clicking his fingers. Suddenly William was flying once more and Brian was talking again.

"It's the motorway travel that gets you," he said. "D'you find that, Arthur?"

My father's eyes were still fixed on mine. "Fortunately," he said, "I am about to retire."

12

CHAPTER TWO

Like . . . Forever?

After my father had left, I told Brian that I needed to think. I walked out of the little house that I had come to love and down the High Street towards St Barnabas School.

Home. The Kingdom of Paranormal Magic and Utter Eternal Mystery. Hardly a day passed without my thinking about it. I missed seeing my sisters and swapping spell recipes with them and hearing all the latest gossip from the paranormal world.

On the other hand, there were my friends from Class Five at St Barnabas. As I walked towards the school, I thought of all the adventures I had been through with them. "I go wherever magic is needed," I had told them when I first met them in the days when they were younger and belonged to Class Three.

Since then, they had helped me as often as I had helped them. Every time when some little problem had occurred – like getting arrested by the police, or losing myself in history, or being turned into a doormat by my evil sister Barbara – my friends from St Barnabas had come to the rescue. Sometimes, to tell the truth, I felt that they were more grown-up than I am.

Still deep in thought, I approached the school gates just as the bell, marking the end of lessons for the day, began to ring. I noticed that some of the parents were waiting for their children so I stayed on the far side of the road. It was a bad time to be recognized.

I watched as some of my old friends – Carl, Nabila, Lizzie, Shelley Kelly – were greeted by their mums or dads and began to make their way home. Suddenly, it seemed to me that it had been a bad idea to come to St Barnabas; I turned and began walking away from the school.

"Yo! Ms Wiz!"

I heard a familiar voice and Jack Beddows appeared beside me, his hair dishevelled, and his shirt hanging out. The school bag slung over his shoulder looked as if it had just been used as a football.

Jack was beckoning across the road where I saw Caroline and Podge emerging through the gates. "It's Ms Wiz," he yelled.

Moments later, Caroline was

running across the zebra crossing,
followed, more slowly, by Podge,
whose mouth was full of chocolate,
as usual.

"How are you doing, Ms Wiz?"
Jack asked as we made our way
towards the High Street.

"Not too terrible," I said.

Caroline peered up at me. "You
look a bit worn out, if you don't mind
my saying so," she said.

"Worn out? Me?" I laughed but the crack in my voice gave me away.

"What is it?" Podge asked. He looked at me quizzically. "What's happened?"

"I have some news," I said.

We sat, the four of us, side by side, on a park bench.

"Do you remember how you have

occasionally asked me where I come from?" I began.

"Yeah," said Jack. "And you always come up with the same totally annoying answer about telling us when the time is right."

"Now is that time," I said quietly. "The place where I come from is a strange place where nothing and no one are quite what they seem."

"Sounds like my house," said Jack.

"Its name is—" I hesitated, uncertain as to whether I should give away my secret "—The Kingdom of Paranormal Magic and Utter Eternal Mystery."

"Snappy name," Jack muttered.

"That is where the Wisdom family lives," I said. "There are twenty sisters. Most of us have been sent to different parts of the world to bring magical help to what we call 'normals'

– people like you."

Jack laughed. "That's the first time Podge has been called—"

"Now I have been summoned back," I interrupted. "My father has told me I must return to the Kingdom of Paranormal Magic and Utter Eternal Mystery with my little William."

For a moment, they looked at me in silence.

"Like . . . forever?" asked Podge.

I nodded my head.

"Can't you just say no?" asked Caroline.

"Yeah," said Jack. "No one tells Ms Wiz what to do. Not even her dad."

"He's not just my dad," I said. "He also happens to be the king."

"The *king*?" All three of them spoke at once.

"But, Ms Wiz, you don't believe in

the monarchy," said Caroline.
"You've always said that we are all
equal and giving someone a special
name does not make them better
than you."

"I know I said that," I agreed.
"That's why I never mentioned to
you that I'm a princess. It didn't seem
important."

"You, a princess? Now you *are*
kidding us," said Jack.

I shook my head. "My precise title
is Her Royal Highness Princess
Dolores of the Kingdom of
Paranormal Magic and Utter Eternal
Mystery."

Jack seemed to find this rather
funny. "No wonder you call yourself
Ms Wiz," he said.

"And now," I said miserably, "my
dad wants me to be queen."

"Wow!" said Podge. "Queen Wiz."

"It's terrible," I said. "I'll have to boss people around and make sure they treat me with respect and spend all my life using my incredible power to make sure that everybody's doing things that please me. And that's just not like me, is it?"

For some reason, the children were staring at their shoes. "No, Ms Wiz," said Caroline eventually. "That really doesn't sound like you at all."

"I don't know how you're going to manage it," said Podge, who seemed to be trying to keep a straight face. "You've never bossed anyone around in your life."

Suddenly I felt my eyes pricking with tears. "The trouble is I like it here. I love seeing you all and having adventures. I'm even getting used to your jokes."

The four of us sat staring gloomily

across the park for a few moments.

Jack clicked his fingers as if he had just had a brilliant idea. "You go back to your land of utter amazing whatever and you tell it straight to your dad that no way is old Muggins here going to be queen. You say to him, 'If you want to retire, kingy – you get one of the other sisters to do it'."

I lowered my head. "I wouldn't

dare," I said quietly.

"Not even if your mates from Class Five were there to back you up?" asked Caroline.

"Nice one, Caro," said Jack. "We could tell the king that we're not going to let you go."

I looked at them and smiled. "You'd have to step outside time," I said. "We'd need to travel a million miles beyond the outer reaches of the known universe. You would be the only normals in the Kingdom of Paranormal Magic and Utter Eternal Mystery."

"And," said Podge, "where, exactly, is the problem?"

I smiled. "Do any of you get travel sickness?" I asked.

One after another they shook their heads.

"Close your eyes and hold on very tightly to the bench," I said, as the humming noise grew louder. "It is about to take you farther than any normal has travelled before."

"Will we be back in time for tea?" asked Podge. "I'm starv—"

And we were gone.

CHAPTER THREE

Going Native

The old home looked the same. When we opened our eyes, our park bench was on a long green lawn. The sun was shining gently and the sound of birdsong was in the air. Ahead of us, surrounded by trees, was a big, rambling old house with roses climbing up the front. From inside could be heard the laughter of children.

"This is my home," I said. "What d'you think?

Podge, Caroline and Jack stood looking at it for a moment.

"It's not what I imagined," said Podge, eventually. "I was expecting a big old castle on the edge of a cliff with eagles flying between the spooky towers."

"It's just a house," said Jack. "A very old house."

Caroline seemed to be waking from a dream. "Well, I think it's lovely," she said walking towards the steps which led up to the front door. "It may not look weird or magic, but it's perfect."

"It's up to the ruler of the kingdom to decide what the Palace of Wisdom should look like. In the past it's been a castle, a rabbit burrow and a tropical island. My father's a traditional type. He likes it like this."

Jack was looking around him. "So, where's the Kingdom of Utter Eternity?" he asked. "All I can see are trees and fields and stuff."

"The kingdom is all around us and also within us," I said. "We take our eternal mystery wherever we go. We are together and yet alone. We are here, now, and yet we are also the past and the future. We are all masters and yet we are all servants."

"What, even when you're queen?" asked Jack.

I thought for a moment before correcting myself. "We are all masters and yet all of us, except one, are servants."

I opened the front door. In the Great Hall, two of the children could be seen flying from one beam to another. One of my uncles was in a big leather chair, sipping a cup of fire. The piano was playing "Nelly the Elephant", all by itself. A group of rats were chatting in a corner. It was as if I had never been away.

"This is such a strange place," Podge murmured.

"All homes are strange in their own way," I said.

"Except most of them don't have talking rats, self-playing pianos, fire-eaters and flying children," observed Caroline.

No one had seemed to notice us, so I walked through the hall, followed by Jack, Podge and Caroline. When we reached a great oak door at the end, I knocked firmly three times and entered.

My father was behind his desk. His eyes were closed and his head was resting sideways on the wing of a high-backed chair.

"Behold the king upon his throne," I said softly.

"Where are all his pages and foot-servants and courtiers?" Caroline whispered.

"In the Kingdom of Paranormal

Magic and Utter Eternal Mystery, we don't need them." I approached the desk and said, "Father."

His eyes opened slowly. When he saw that I was there, he sat up sharply. "Yes, that's right, do that," he barked, and straightened up in the chair. "Ah, Dolores, I've just been doing some work."

"In your dreams," muttered Podge.

"Exactly, dreamwork can be extraordinarily useful, I find." For the first time, my father noticed that I was not alone.

"Who are these young people?" he asked.

"Your Majesty, this is Jack Beddows, Caroline Thompson and Peter Harris, who prefers to be called Podge."

"Welcome to you all," said the king.

"Bow to the king," I muttered out

of the corner of my mouth.

"You what?" said Jack.

There was nothing for it. I took a deep breath and the humming noise was all around us. As if a great invisible hand had thwacked them on their backs, the three of them fell forward on their faces.

"Please, please." My father laughed modestly. "There is absolutely no need to abase yourselves before me.

I'm only a king, after all. What very nicely brought-up children you are."

"Yes, aren't we," grumbled Caroline as she stood up and dusted herself down.

"I shall assign them magical duties this afternoon," said my father. "Which spells are your specialities, my dears?"

"We don't exactly do magic," said Jack.

"Don't do magic?" The king looked surprised. "How very odd."

"They're—" I hesitated, concerned how my father would take the news. "Well, actually, they're normals, Father."

"Normals?" The king looked slightly surprised. "Oh well, I'm sure they'll learn soon enough. Welcome to the Kingdom of Paranormal Magic and Utter Eternal Mystery. I'm sure you'll be very happy here."

There was an awkward silence.
"Actually—" It was Jack who spoke.
"We're only visiting."

"We have families to get back to,"
said Caroline.

"And food," said Podge. "It's
teatime."

"Father, I'm just here briefly," I
said. "I need to discuss something
with you." I turned to Jack, Caroline
and Podge. "Would you like to
explore the house?"

They looked uncertain.

"Or would you prefer to stay here,
frozen in time?"

"Let's go," said Jack.

"Your Majesty, I have a problem," I
said a few moments later when I was
alone with my father. I took a deep

breath. "The fact is, I'm happy where I am."

He smiled. "Of course you are. And we're very happy to see you, too."

"I mean that I'm happy there – with the normals, looking after little William, being with my husband Brian."

"William can come with you and Brian can visit any time he wants."

"Then there's Class Five at St Barnabas School."

My father frowned. "And what exactly has Class Five at St Barnabas School got to offer which cannot be found in the Kingdom of Paranormal Magic and Utter Eternal Mystery?"

I sat down in seat in front of his desk and spoke about some of the things I had done with Class Five. I told him about Herbert running up the school inspector's trousers, about the time I turned everyone in the Houses of Parliament into monkeys, about when I became a doctor and a head teacher and the occasion when I ended up reading the news on television. I talked about becoming a supermodel, going back in time, falling in love with the most famous film star in Hollywood, Brad Le Touquet. I even revealed that my evil twin sister had captured Podge, taken him deep into the underworld and turned him into a zombie slave.

"That Barbara." My father chuckled. "She always was a bit flighty."

"What I'm trying to say is that I'd miss all that," I said. "I don't think I'm quite ready to be queen."

"You've gone native, that's your problem. I've seen it many times

before. Often when a paranormal operative spends too much time among normals, she starts wanting to be normal herself."

"Maybe someone else could be queen for a while. One of the other sisters or—" I hesitated "—Mother."

The king looked away quickly as if he had noticed something terribly interesting in the garden outside the

window. "Your mother appears to find the continent of Africa more interesting than her husband," he said quietly. "I have not seen her for over a year."

I sighed. "So there's no one else, then?"

My father squared his shoulders. "I am your king and this is my command," he said. "Go to the

Operations Room. Visit some of your sisters and talk to them about this. I shall need a decision from you by the end of today."

I stood up, gave a quick curtsey and made for the door. "Thanks, Dad," I called out over my shoulder.

CHAPTER FOUR

Dumped Big-Time by the Frothies

There was no time to lose, but when I emerged from my father's study there was no sign of Jack, Caroline or Podge. As soon as I started looking for them through the house, aunts and uncles noticed me and wanted to chat while children pestered me for new spells.

Some of the rats scampered after me, asking for the latest news of Herbert. Eventually, to shut them up, I told them about his marrying a street-rat called Arabella and that they had thirty-two children. "Probably thirty-six by now," I added. "I haven't seen him for a couple of hours."

Leaving the rats muttering among themselves about this news, I went outside. There, on the croquet lawn, some of the children of the palace were teaching Jack how to fly, laughing as he spread his arms and made his first nervous flights.

"Spells are for later," I said briskly. "We have to fly around the world in the next few hours."

As I spoke, Jack landed in a crumpled heap on the grass. "Around the world?" he said. "I can only just get off the ground."

But I was on my way back to the house. "Follow me," I said.

"She's behaving like she's queen already," muttered Caroline.

I took them through the hall. Under the stairs was a heavy metal door against which I placed my hand. It opened slowly and we descended the forty-nine steps to the Operations Room.

It was a small circular room with screens on every wall. "This is the nerve centre of the kingdom," I said. "From here, we can track what every paranormal operative is doing."

I pressed a button near the door. The lights lowered and all the screens lit up.

"Wow!" said Jack. "It's the ultimate telly room. Can we watch *The Simpsons*?"

"You are now surrounded by my family," I said. "In the next few hours, we have to find which of my sisters could be queen instead of me."

"Can we get a takeaway pizza while we watch?" asked Podge. "My stomach's begging for mercy."

Caroline was looking from screen to screen. "They're all doing different things and they all look exactly like you," she said.

"Isn't it a bit embarrassing being watched all the time?" asked Jack. "What about when you want to be private – like when you go to the toilet?"

"Grow up, Jack," said Caroline. "Paranormal operatives don't go to the toilet."

"Maybe they have magic, invisible loos," said Jack. "And when they—"

"Stop it, stop it, stop it!" I shouted. "Here we are, facing the biggest moment in my entire life as a paranormal operative and all you can talk about is . . . ablutions." I turned to one of the screens where Ludmilla Wizgova could be seen climbing a mountain with a group of normals. "I don't think she's suitable to be queen somehow."

"Do we just talk to them through the screen?" asked Podge.

"No, we visit them. One tap on the screen and we'll be transported to whichever part of the world they are in. The only question is, who to visit? We only have time to see three of them."

I looked at one screen after another. My family certainly seemed to be

having a good time out there.

"Hey, surfing," Jack called out from the other side of the room. "Take a look at that—" He reached out towards the screen.

"Jack! Look out!" I shouted.

But it was too late. There was a muffled explosion and a blinding flash of flame. When we were able to open our eyes again, the only sign of Jack in the Operations Room was a small plume of smoke.

I glanced at the screen where he had been standing. Across some golden sands, I saw my sister Ms Wazza walking beside a tall, broad-shouldered man in torn-off jeans who had a surfboard under his arm. Running behind them was Jack Beddows.

I sighed. I had a few moments to find a new queen for the Kingdom of Paranormal Magic and Utter Eternal Mystery and Jack had transported himself to the other side of the world. "It looks like our first trip is to Australia," I said.

"Australia!" Caroline clapped her hands. "Can we see where they make *Neighbours*? Will there be kangaroos? And koalas? I love koalas."

"Will we back in time for tea?" asked Podge.

"Give me your hands," I said. I touched the screen, there was a flash and suddenly we were sitting on a beach, blinking at the brightness of the sun.

"And a very g'day to you, mates," said my sister Ms Wazza. "Nice of you to fly in."

I stood up, brushing the sand off my jeans. "Hullo, Scarlett," I said, kissing her on her tanned cheek. "These are my friends Caroline, Podge and Jack."

"Hi," she said. "Welcome to Byron Bay, choicest spot in the wide brown. This is my mate Clyde. We're looking for the perfect wave. We caught an absolute beaut up the coast but we're getting dumped big-time by the frothies on this stretch, y'know?"

Jack, Caroline and Podge looked confused. Scarlett frowned. "Don't these kids speak English, Sis?" she asked.

"Yes, but it's slightly different English from yours," I said. "I was under the impression that you were in Australia for magical purposes."

Scarlett laughed. "Good old Dolly." She winked at Clyde. "She always was the goody-two-shoes of the family." She turned back to me. "I did a few spells back in town. Now I'm chilling out with my mates, trying to use some magic to hold up a wave so that it carries me right across Byron Bay."

"That sounds great," said Jack. "Could I have a go?"

Clyde dropped his surfboard on to the sand. "No worries, I'll give the kid a few lessons on dry land and then—"

"I think not," I said briskly. I drew

47

a double circle in the sand around Jack, Caroline and Podge. "We're off back to the Operations Room."

"But Ms Wiz—" Jack began to protest, but I held up a hand and stepped into the circle.

"Nice to meet you, Clyde," I said. "And Scarlett, if I were you, I'd put in a bit of paranormal work down here, otherwise you might get sent somewhere else in the world." I smiled coldly. "I've heard that Siberia's free."

"No drama," Scarlett muttered. "I might get back to town to cast a spell or two right now."

I whispered, "Operations . . . " and by the time, I had added " . . . Room," we were back home.

Caroline looked around her. "All right, Ms Wiz. I have to admit it – I'm dead impressed."

I shrugged. "Travelling around the world's easy when you know how," I said.

"Not the travelling," said Caroline. "It was the way you took hold of the situation. Scarlett really looked up to you."

"Between you and me, I don't think she was queen material," said Jack.

I looked around the screens. "Well spotted, Jack," I said. "But who is?"

"How about this one?" asked Caroline. "She seems to be in charge of some sort of circus."

"Not a bad idea," I said. "Her name's Ms 用 邪 法 个 女 人."

"Er, 用 邪 法 个 女 人?" said Jack.

I moved towards the screen. "You can call her Wiz Phu, for short."

CHAPTER FIVE

Hello Dolly

We were in a gigantic circus tent. High above our heads, a girl was doing some exercises on a tightrope. A family of jugglers were throwing swords to one another while, on the other side of the circus ring, two clowns were going through a custard-pie routine.

In the centre of the ring stood a woman in riding gear, carrying a whip which she was cracking now and then. It was my sister, Wiz Phu, and she was bossing people around, as usual.

"No, no, no! You're falling before the pie hits you," she was shouting at the clowns. "Try it again."

"Wiz Phu?" I spoke gently.

Wiz Phu glanced towards me. "Hey, welcome, Sister. Good to see you," she said, as if we ran into each other every day of the week. "Step out of the ring, will you? I won't be more than an hour."

I stood my ground. "We haven't got an hour," I said. "I need to talk to you about something very important."

Wiz Phu laughed angrily. "Something more important than the *Wiz Phu Circus of Magic and Mystery* which happens to be playing in Beijing next Monday? Somehow I'd be surprised." She looked at Caroline, Jack and Podge. "Who are these children?" she barked. "Have they got permits? Strangers are banned from the rehearsal area."

Caroline moved closer to me. "Your

sister's dead scary," she murmured.

"Come to think of it, you kids can make yourselves useful," said Wiz Phu. "Tell me if you think this is funny." She screamed at the clowns, who were standing, dripping with custard, to carry on. One of them picked up another pie. Holding it high in the air, he walked towards the other clown. Just as he approached, he tripped. Custard flew everywhere.

"Well?" Wiz Phu glowered at the children. "Was that funny? Did it really make you laugh?"

"Yeah, ha ha," said Jack, straight-faced. "It . . . cracked me up."

"I almost split my sides," said Caroline nervously.

"What about you?" Wiz Phu asked Podge.

"I was wondering if you had any spare custard pies," he said. "It was such a great act I'd like to practise at home."

Wiz Phu seemed to relax and turned to me. "What was it you wanted to ask me, Dolly?"

I was tracing a double circle in the sand around myself, Jack, Caroline and Podge. I smiled at my sister. "Nothing," I said quietly. "I've changed my mind."

Back in the Operations Room, the four of us gazed at the screens around us.

"Boy, am I glad St Barnabas got you," Jack said eventually. "Your sisters are all nutters. Ms Wazza just thought about herself and Wiz Phu was like the most power-crazed teacher there's ever been."

"You were so good with them." Caroline smiled at me. "I reckon they're lucky to have someone like you as a sister."

I walked slowly around the screens. As I looked at my nineteen sisters, I realized that, much as I loved them, not one of them was going to be able to take charge of the Kingdom of Paranormal Magic and Utter Eternal Mystery. On the last screen, I watched an older woman. She was sitting under a big shady tree, surrounded by little African children.

"It's our last chance," I said. "You are about to meet my mother."

I held out my hand towards the screen.

"Well, hello, Dolly!"

The face that I loved, but had not seen for a long time, looked up from the book she was reading and smiled

as if she had been expecting me.
"Come over and join us under the
baobab tree."

The four of us picked our way
through the children. I kissed Mother
and introduced her to Caroline,
Podge and Jack. She stood up and
addressed her class. "This is my
daughter and her friends," she said.
"Her name is Ms Wiz. So, what do
you say to her?"

"Good morning, Ms Wiz," the class

said in unison.

"Now I know she would love to tell us all about her life," said my mother, "because she's a teacher, too. Only she does her paranormal magic in a faraway land."

I smiled. "I promise I'll come back to talk to you," I told the African children. "But right now I've got to have a quick talk with my mum."

Mother handed out picture books to her class and told them to read to themselves under a nearby tree. When they had settled down, she said, "Well, what would you like to do while you're here? See around the village? Watch the animals at the waterhole?"

"There's no time, Mum," I said. "I've come to talk to you about Dad."

My mother sighed. "I suppose he's as busy as ever, running his blessed kingdom."

"He misses you," I said.

"And I miss him. But I had to come out here to do this for myself. All I used to be was the king's wife. Now I'm being myself. I'm putting magic to good use."

"He wants to retire, Mum. He thinks it's time someone else took over."

My mother clapped her hands, almost as if she were a little girl. "That's wonderful news. He'll have more time to spend with me. If I came back, we could be just Mr and Mrs Wisdom again." She closed her eyes. "No more running the kingdom morning, noon and night. What bliss that would be."

I hesitated and, in that moment, I knew that I had been wrong to think that my mother could be queen. She needed a rest as well. It was time for her to be a grandmother. "I know he'd really like that, too," I said.

"And that was what you came to tell me? That Dad wants me to come back? How sweet of you, dear."

By now Jack, Caroline and Podge were staring at me. I knew that they understood why I had changed my mind.

"Yes," I said. "That's why I came. I'll tell Dad you'll be back as soon as you've said goodbye to your class."

I stood up and carefully drew a double circle in the earth.

"There was one other thing, Dolly." My mother was frowning. "If your father is descending from the throne, who is going to take over from him?"

"Oh, didn't I tell you?" I smiled. "I am."

CHAPTER SIX

Prince Brian

We travelled through time and space but now our destination was not the Kingdom of Paranormal Magic and Utter Eternal Mystery. The two circles that I had traced around us when we were under a baobab tree in Africa took us home to a park bench in St Barnabas Park.

Jack scratched his head. "Er, Ms Wiz," he said, "was that a dream or have we just been to the Kingdom of Magical Utterly Utterness, met your dad, who happens to be king, popped over to Australia and then China before seeing your mum in Africa?"

"Dream? Reality? Magic? Truth?" I smiled. "What, at the end of the day, do they all mean?"

"At the end of the day, it's the end of the day and that means it's past my teatime," grumbled Podge. "If we stepped out of time, how come I'm getting hungrier all the time?"

"Paranormal magic has great power," I explained. "But there are some things that are too powerful for it to control – the weather, life and death, mighty earthquakes, the tides

of the oceans. And the appetite of Podge Harris. Your stomach is a force of Nature."

I noticed for the first time that Caroline was staring sadly across the park. "It wasn't a dream, was it, Ms Wiz?" she said quietly. "You've decided to become queen."

"Not queen exactly," I said. "I believe that we are all equal and that giving someone a special name does not make them better than you. I'll probably call myself something simple and humble like 'Her Royal Highness'."

"HRH Ms Wiz," said Jack. "I've heard it all now."

"That means you'll be leaving," said Caroline. "You'll be so busy running your kingdom that you won't have time for a little class from St Barnabas."

I put my arm around her. "One of the great things about being a royal highness is that I can do exactly what I like," I said. "So I can come and visit you now and then. I can even invite you back to the Palace of Wisdom if you feel like stepping out of time again."

"I'll make sure I bring my lunch box next time," muttered Podge.

I stood up. "It's time for us to go back to our families," I said. "I have one last favour to ask of you. I'd like all my friends to gather in the school playground at noon tomorrow – children, parents, teachers, even PC Boote."

"How can we arrange that?" asked Caroline.

I smiled. "Class Five can do anything it sets its mind to," I said.

"There could be a fire alarm," said

Jack. "And the parents could have been summoned to see Mr Gilbert. And an emergency call just might have been put through to PC Boote at the police station. These things could just happen."

"We'd better get going," said Caroline more cheerfully. "We've got some calls to make."

The three of them stood in front of me. "I'll see you tomorrow at noon," I said. "Thanks for helping me make up my mind. I don't know how I'm going to reign without you." I kissed them quickly, one after the other.

"We'll be there whenever some Class Five magic is needed," said Caroline.

I laughed. I watched them as they made their way out of the park. At the gate, they turned and each of them waved once more. It was time to go

back to the house. I needed to talk to
Herbert, and then to Brian.

"Sorry, old bean. Not a chance. I
wouldn't dream of moving."

Herbert was sitting on his chair as
four of his children scrambled all
over him. He held in his paws a
picture book called *Ratman* which he
was trying to read to them. On the
carpet nearby, lying on her side, his
wife Arabella was feeding five babies.
Their other twenty or so children
were playing rat games elsewhere
in the room, running up curtains,
nibbling the edge of the carpet and
playing hide-and-seek in the chest of
drawers.

"The Palace of Wisdom is our true
home," I said. "You may like it here
but you're a magic rat. You belong in

the land of magic."

Herbert raised his little arm as if he were a policeman holding up the traffic. "Speak to the paw. The head ain't listening," he said. "Now, where were we, children?" He returned to his book and started reading, "Is it a bird? Is it a plane? No, it's Ratman!"

"The choice is yours, Herbert," I said. "You either come home and spend your life chatting with the other rats and doing spells. Or you stay here and become an ordinary street rat – rummaging around dustbins and living in a sewer."

Herbert gave a little shudder. "I don't think dustbins and sewers are quite me somehow," he said.

At that moment, Arabella looked up and gave him a wide, yellow-toothed smile.

"But what about my other half?"

Herbert asked, dropping his voice as if Arabella could understand what he was saying. "She wouldn't exactly be at home with all that magic. She's a rat normal. She can't even talk."

"I can sort that out," I said. "I'll give her a voice. I am going to be queen after all."

"Hmm." Herbert pondered for a moment. "But what will she be like when she can talk? I mean, between you and me, she might be . . . well, you know, NQOCD – not quite our class, darling."

I was going to tell Herbert that it didn't matter how people spoke, that it was what they said that mattered, when I had a better idea. Humming filled the room, and Arabella started as if suddenly awakening from a deep, deep sleep. She looked up at Herbert.

"What is that *ghaaastly* book you're reading, darling?" Arabella's voice was high-pitched and squeaky, like a chalk on blackboard. "I always hoped our little ones would learn to read by looking at *Vogue*. Taste and manners are *sooo* important in the young."

I winced. There had been no way of telling what Arabella would be like when she had a voice. It turned out that she was an even bigger snob than her husband.

But, to my relief, Herbert was smiling as he put aside his copy of *Ratman*. "Darling, I've just had the most marvellous idea," he said. "How would you like to move house?"

Leaving Herbert and Arabella to make plans for their new life, I made

my way downstairs.

Brian was in the kitchen, feeding William who was in his high chair. I kissed them both, carefully avoiding the food around the Wiz Kid's mouth, and sat at the table, watching them for a moment, my husband and my little boy.

"I've been to see my father," I said.

"Arthur?" said Brian. "How was

he? Still flying around as a bird,
pretending to be a king?"

"Sort of," I said. "D'you remember
I told you that he was going to
retire?"

Brian nodded. "I do seem to recall
something of that nature," he said.

"Well." I took a deep breath. "King
Arthur told me that he would like
me to be supreme ruler of the

Kingdom of Paranormal Magic and Utter Eternal Mystery."

Brian spooned another helping into William's mouth. "That would be quite a promotion," he said eventually. "What a shame you can't accept."

When I said nothing, he looked up sharply. "You can't accept, Dolores, can you?"

"I have to go home," I said quietly. "William needs to be among magical children like himself. It's his destiny."

"And what about my destiny?"

"You could come too. You would be Prince Consort to me – Prince Brian."

Brian laid the spoon down. William waved his arms. The spoon lifted off the plate, dipped into the food,

hovered upwards and carefully fed
him.

"I don't want to be a prince," he
said, almost as if he were talking to
himself. "I like being a school
inspector. I have lots of work to do
here."

As William fed himself, I spoke
about my journey home. I told Brian
how I had travelled around the world

with Jack, Caroline and Podge. I spoke about my father and my mother. Like the Wiz Kid, I too had my destiny to fulfil.

When I had finished, Brian thought for a moment. "You took those children from Class Five with you?" he asked. "And they didn't have to become paranormal operatives?"

I shook my head. "Jack had a go at flying but basically they were the same as ever. We just stepped out of time. When we came back, it was as if we had never been away."

"I see."

"You could do that, too." I spoke softly. "You could be prince consort one day, school inspector the next. You would have two homes, and two lives for the price of one."

Brian gazed out of the window.

When he looked back at me, he was smiling. "Now *that* sounds like a bargain," he said.

CHAPTER SEVEN

The Rat Carriage

Why is there always a fuss whenever
I decide to do something? There was
a fuss when I arrived at St Barnabas
and did some magic, as if turning
teachers into farmyard animals was
somehow "unnatural". There was a
fuss among the paranormal
operatives when I fell in love with
Dracula and decided to marry him.
There were other fusses when I
became Prime Minister, visited the
underworld and lost a couple of
classes when I was head teacher.

But now there was the biggest fuss
of all.

Back in the Kingdom of Paranormal
Magic and Eternal Mystery, when I

returned to my father's study, I found my parents sitting together, holding hands.

"Thanks to you," my father smiled happily, "my dear wife has returned from Africa. Now all that I need to complete my contentment is to see you crowned as the new queen."

And that was where the fuss began. I told my father that I would be honoured to become the new ruler but that I would have a coronation without a crown or dressing-up or parades with massed brass bands or angels flying over the palace in "V" formation or being brought to the throne in a giant rat carriage or having the children dressed up in velvet and lace or any of that usual royal stuff.

"What is more, Father," I said, "I shall not allow myself to be called the queen. I shall simply be HRH

Ms Wiz."

The king seemed to sink in his chair. "Oh, Dolores." He buried his face in his hands. "Why do you always have to be different?"

"I'm not different. That's exactly the point. What I believe is that we are all equal and that giving someone a special name does not make them better than you."

"But you *are* different, Dolly," my mother said in her most reasonable voice. "You're the supreme ruler."

"And if that's the case," I countered, "I'd like everything in the kingdom to be modern and fair-minded."

"But the people at the palace like a bit of a show now and then," said my father. "It's the old Wisdom tradition. In many ways, paranormals are very normal."

"Well, it's time they grew up," I said firmly. "All this bowing and scraping is old-fashioned and downright embarrassing. It is time for the spirit of change to reach the kingdom, for old Wisdom to make way for new Wiz."

My father squared his shoulders and gazed seriously into my eyes. "I am your father," he said. "I am also your king. This is my decree."

For the first time in thousands of years, I stared back at the king and refused to bow my head. "Well, Dad," I said quietly, "put it this way. It's new Wiz or no Wiz."

There was a moment of tense silence. Then, to my surprise, my father began to laugh quietly. "You're going to be quite a queen," he said.

"HRH."

He nodded his head, still smiling. "Quite an HRH," he said.

So we agreed to meet each other halfway on the question of the coronation.

The ceremony would take place in the Glade of Majesty, deep in the woods, as is traditional. I agreed that the mighty host of paranormal operatives could be present as usual

80

but instead of being dressed in gold and silver with traditional peacock and raven feather accessories, the dress code would be "smart casual". I refused to wear the crown – a ridiculous, towering thing of priceless jewels which would make my neck ache – but agreed to accept a simple diamond tiara. The brass band would be there but, instead of playing the aggressive marching tunes that were traditional on these occasions, they would play a medley of Abba hits. There would be a fly-past but, rather than being restricted to angels, anyone from the kingdom who fancied a bit of a fly could join in.

There was something of a problem with the rat carriage. In the past, the rats of the palace joined paws and generally tangled up together in a very complicated and beautiful way to make a royal carriage, which would bear the future monarch across the lawn to the Glade of Majesty. When I told the rats that I thought that the sight of a person, even an HRH, lying back in a carriage made out of their own bodies was an insult to rodent dignity, they told me that they had been rehearsing for this day for years.

In the end, I agreed that the carriage would proceed as usual but on one condition – Herbert and Arabella would sit with me to show that, during the reign of HRH Ms Wiz, rats and paranormal operatives would live as equals.

As for the ceremony itself, I insisted on new Wiz wording. The king was reluctant to agree, some of the sisters threatened not to show up, but, in the end, I calmed their fears. I told them that, in the Kingdom of Paranormal Magic and Utter Eternal Mystery, we had always believed in change – after all, our magic was changing things all the time. Now it was time for us to change, too.

And there was something else that I did – something so unusual that I could tell absolutely no one about it. The day before the coronation, I flew once around the forest glade, spreading sand as I went. Then I flew around once more, tracing two lines in the sand.

At this great moment, the coronation of their new HRH, the people of the Kingdom of Paranormal Magic and Utter Eternal Mystery would be in for a surprise.

Chapter Eight

Dancing Queen

The sun was shining on the day that I would become the ruler of all that is magic and paranormal. A hum of excitement hung over the woods surrounding the palace as crowds gathered for the coronation.

At a few moments after eleven o'clock, the procession emerged from the gates of the palace courtyard. Behind the flag-bearer stood my father, smiling at my mother by his side. They moved towards the lawn, followed by my sisters who walked two by two except for Barbara, who stood alone at the back, a look of thunderous jealousy on her face. Then came the band, followed by aunts and uncles of the Wisdom family and special guests from the palace.

Finally, in a majestic carriage of writhing rats whose dark coats seemed to glisten in the morning sun, came me, HRH Ms Wiz. On my right was Herbert, wearing a natty purple waistcoat and spotted bow tie. Beyond him was Arabella, who waved graciously to the crowd as if she were really the one that everyone had come to see. On my left, babbling happily, was William, soon to become Prince Wiz Kid.

We made our way past the palace entrance and the croquet lawn and up the great avenue of trees which leads to the Glade of Majesty. Here the procession halted. As is the tradition, my father was the first to step into the glade. He walked

towards the ancient oak that stands at
its centre. A throne has been carved
out of its trunk, on each side of which
the tree's branches spread like
mighty green wings. My father
ascended the steps of the oak throne
and took his seat.

"I am Arthur," he announced.
"This morning, I am King Wisdom,
Master of Magic, Sire of Spells, Peer
Extraordinaire and Supreme

Sovereign of the Kingdom of
Paranormal Magic and Utter Eternal
Mystery. On the stroke of midday, I
shall be king no more but merely
Arthur Wisdom, citizen. From that
moment, your ruler shall be—" The
king paused and turned his eyes to
me. "Your ruler shall be Dolores, my
beloved daughter."

From the woods all around us,

there was the sound of applause like rain falling on leaves. I alighted from the rat carriage and made my way into the glade, followed by Herbert, Arabella, William, my sisters, aunts and uncles and the members of the palace court.

At this moment of my crowning glory I stood before the throne, my head bowed, my heart thumping with fear and excitement. From the palace behind us, the first chimes of the great clock could be heard. My father stood up, took the three steps downwards and placed the simple tiara on my bowed head. He then kissed me gently on the cheek, and with his hand under my elbow, guided me to the first step. On the sixth chime, he released me. I mounted the steps and turned.

The clock chimed eight, nine, ten . . .

From the forest around us, a low humming noise could be heard. It grew louder and louder.

. . . eleven, twelve.

I raised my hands. The forest was engulfed in a heavy mist. It cleared slowly. The glade was no longer surrounded by trees. The crowd in the woods could no longer be heard. The oak throne, the Glade of Majesty and all who stood in it were in a new place altogether, in a school playground.

"Wow, what a tree house!" shouted a voice that I recognized.

"Its not a tree house." I smiled down on Jack Beddows. "This happens to be my oak throne."

"It's Ms Wiz!" shouted Lizzie. There were cheers from Class Five.

For a few seconds, I enjoyed the strangeness. Close to me, in the

Glade of Majesty, were William, my mother and father, my sisters, Herbert and Arabella. Then beyond, just outside the magic circle, were the people, the normals, with whom I had done so much. At the front of the crowd, I saw Jack, Podge, Lizzie, Caroline, Nabila, Carl, Kelly and all the other children of Class Five. Behind them I saw the school staff – Mr Gilbert, the head teacher, Mr Bailey, Miss Gomaz, Mrs Hicks – and, with them, the librarian, Mr Goff, the local policeman, PC Boote, and some of the parents.

Standing slightly apart from the other adults was my own sweet school inspector husband, Mr Brian Arnold.

I turned to the court before me.

"I, HRH Ms Wiz do solemnly declare—" Before I could go any

further, I was aware of a kerfuffle in the crowd. Mr Gilbert burst into the Glade of Majesty, followed by Mrs Hicks and Miss Gomaz, with PC Boote bringing up the rear.

"You can stop that right now," said the head teacher, puffing slightly. "While we are always happy to see old friends at St Barnabas, it is strictly against school regulations for strangers to enter school premises without written permission."

"Strangers?" I smiled. "These are not strangers. They are my family, the royal dynasty of the Kingdom of Paranormal Magic and Utter Eternal Mystery. This is the crowning of the Mistress of Magic, Dame of Spells, Peer Extraordinaire and Supreme Sovereign of the Kingdom."

"Just listen to her. She thinks she's so special," muttered Mrs Hicks.

"Talk about giving yourself airs," said Miss Gomaz.

PC Boote stepped forward. "There is absolutely no way that tree is legal," he said. "It constitutes a serious safety hazard to the kiddies in this playground."

"But this is my coronation," I protested. "It only happens once every 10,000 years or so. I thought you'd be pleased that I decided to hold it at St Barnabas."

"Regulations are regulations," said PC Boote firmly.

I smiled down from my throne. In the past, my spells had turned teachers into geese and sheep, and once I had turned the staff of an entire police station into rabbits, but this was my special day and I was in a good mood. As a distant humming noise could be heard in the playground, I put a love spell on them.

Suddenly, Mr Gilbert seemed to forget all about me. He turned to Miss Gomaz. "Why, Miss Gomaz, you're . . . beautiful," he said, blinking up at the teacher.

Mrs Hicks had grabbed PC Boote's hand. "You know I've always found

men in uniforms fearfully attractive," she said.

"Oh, please, Ms Wiz," Podge shouted from the front row. "This could get seriously embarrassing."

I raised my hands once more. Silence descended on the crowd.

"I, HRH Ms Wiz, do solemnly declare— " I glanced across at Class Five. "I solemnly swear that I am not going to change one bit," I said. "I have always said that I would go wherever magic is needed. Right now, magic is needed in my own kingdom and that is where I shall be."

There were mutterings of disappointment from the class.

"But—" I paused for a moment. "All my friends from St Barnabas will be welcome to visit me at any time. My beloved husband Brian Arnold will be moving from one world to the other. All you need to do is contact him."

There were cheers from Class Five.

Brian smiled up at me and it was at that moment that a low rumbling hum seemed to fill the air. The oak throne where I was sitting rose slightly off the ground and soon the entire Glade of Majesty, with my family, Herbert and Arabella, seemed to hover in the air above the playground. Behind me, the band struck up with my favourite Abba song "Dancing Queen".

Above the noise, I noticed that Podge seemed to be shouting something. He pointed desperately at Mr Gilbert and Miss Gomaz, who were still in each others' arms. Beyond them PC Boote was walking hand in hand with Mrs Hicks towards the school gates.

"Whoops." I remembered the love spell. Smiling, I pointed to Mr Gilbert and Miss Gomaz. They sprang apart, as if suddenly realizing what they were doing. Mrs Hicks stood back from PC Boote, arms crossed. They were once again the way they used to be. Everyone at St Barnabas was the same as I had always known them.

We were getting fainter now and, to my surprise, I noticed that my eyes had filled with tears. I gazed downwards at Class Five and, through the blur, they smiled up at me from the playground as if they were a single, friendly face.

I waved my hand and slowly, slowly, they began to fade from sight.

The Wiz Kid was crawling up the steps of the oak throne. I picked him up and held him to me.

At last, the time had come – we were going home.